I Am AMAZING!

BY Alissa Holder & Zulekha Holder-Young   ILLUSTRATED BY Nneka Myers

FLAMINGO BOOKS

FLAMINGO BOOKS
An imprint of Penguin Random House LLC, New York

First published in the United States of America by Flamingo Books,
an imprint of Penguin Random House LLC, 2022

Visit us online at penguinrandomhouse.com.

Library of Congress Cataloging-in-Publication Data is available.

Printed in the United States of America

ISBN 9780593327326

1 3 5 7 9 10 8 6 4 2

PC

Design by Opal Roengchai
Text set in Gill Sans Alt One Book
This art was rendered in Procreate for iPad and Photoshop with lots of love!

For our dad, Allister Holder.
You taught us to be our own superheroes,
when you were ours all along.
Forever in our hearts.
—Ali's Angels

To my family and friends, who are all everyday superheroes!
—N. M.

WHOOSH! Boom!

Ayaan slid down the slide.

Zoom! Ayaan whizzed by
his friends on the swings.
Mia was flying high,

but Aria needed a push.
Ayaan was there in a flash.

Look! By the rock wall!

Elijah and Atara need a hand.

Ayaan sprung into action to pull them up.

Amazing Ayaan to the rescue!

Feeling proud, Ayaan climbed
down the rock wall.
As he jumped off, he heard
David and Brian laughing.

Ayaan looked at them and realized
that they were laughing at *him*.

"Ayaan, why are you always running around the playground pretending to be a superhero?" asked Brian.
"You can't be a real superhero," said David.
"You don't look like a superhero to me."

Ayaan took off his cape and
walked slowly back into school.
He wished the day was already over.

After school his dad
knew right away
that something
was wrong.

"What's up, buddy?" he asked. "You don't look happy."

"I left my smile at school today," Ayaan replied.

"Superheroes always carry their smile. Why don't you have yours?" asked his dad.

"I decided today I'm not a superhero anymore.
My friends said that superheroes don't look like me."

Ayaan's dad was quiet for a moment.
Then he looked at his son and spoke very slowly.
"Even though your friends may not have seen
many superheroes that look like you,
superheroes are everywhere.

"Superheroes come in all shapes and sizes.
They don't always wear capes
and they don't fly through the air,
but superheroes are doing important things every day.
Anyone can be a superhero, including you.

"What makes *you* amazing, Ayaan?"

"Well, I'm always kind to my friends . . .

I guess I'm helpful . . .

Sometimes I'm brave,

and when I wear my cape, I feel so strong."

"It's true!" shouted Ayaan's dad.
"You ARE kind.
You are helpful, brave, and strong.
And you know what else?

"You have the biggest heart.
That's what makes you the
best kind of superhero."

Ayaan finally smiled—
and it was a big smile this time.
"I *can* be a superhero!"

He pulled his cape and
mask out of his backpack,
putting them on as
he ran like the wind.

Whoosh! Boom! Down the steps.
Zoom!
Ayaan whizzed through the garden and leapt up onto his favorite rock.

Amazing Ayaan to the rescue!